SILLY BILLY!

SILLY BILLY!

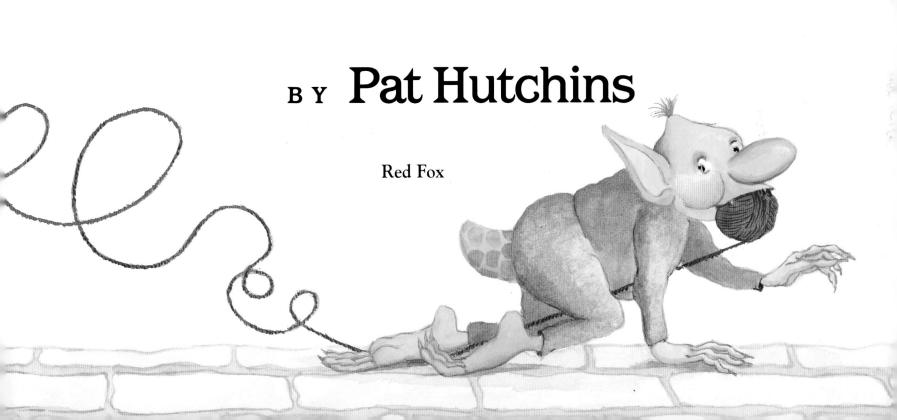

BY **Pat Hutchins**

Red Fox

A Red Fox Book

Published by Random House Children's Books
20 Vauxhall Bridge Road, London SW1V 2SA

A division of Random House UK Ltd
London Melbourne Sydney Auckland
Johannesburg and agencies throughout the world

© Pat Hutchins 1992

First published in the USA 1992
by Greenwillow Books
First published in Great Britain 1992
by Julia MacRae

Red Fox edition 1994

Printed in China

RANDOM HOUSE UK Limited Reg. No. 954009

ISBN 0 09 925561 8

FOR SUSAN HIRSCHMAN!

Hazel was playing a game with Grandpa,
Grandma, and Ma and Pa.
Billy wanted to play, too.

"Let Billy have a turn," said Grandma.

"He's only little."

Billy tossed the board up and threw the cards
into the air.

"SILLY BILLY!" said Hazel. "You've spoiled my
game. I might as well play with my dolls' house."

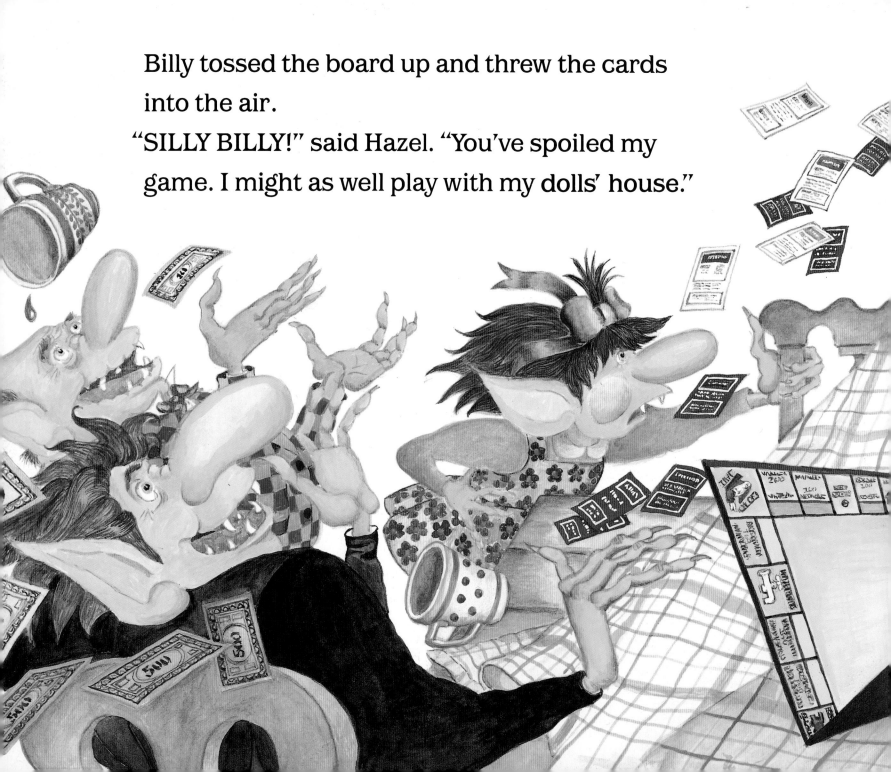

But Billy wanted to play with the dolls' house too.

"Let Billy have a turn," said Grandpa.
"He's only little."

Billy tipped the dolls' house on its side,
and all the furniture fell out.

"SILLY BILLY!" said Hazel. "You've spoiled my game.
I might as well play with the building blocks."

But Billy wanted to play
with the building blocks, too.

"Let Billy have a turn," said Ma.
"He's only little."

Billy knocked all the bricks
down and jumbled them up.
"SILLY BILLY!" said Hazel.
"You've spoiled my game.
I might as well play with the train set."

But Billy wanted to play
with the train set, too.

"Let Billy have a turn," said Pa.
"He's only little."

Billy pulled the tracks to bits
and unhooked the wagons.
"SILLY BILLY!" said Hazel.
"You've spoiled all my games.
I might as well go to sleep in the toy box!"

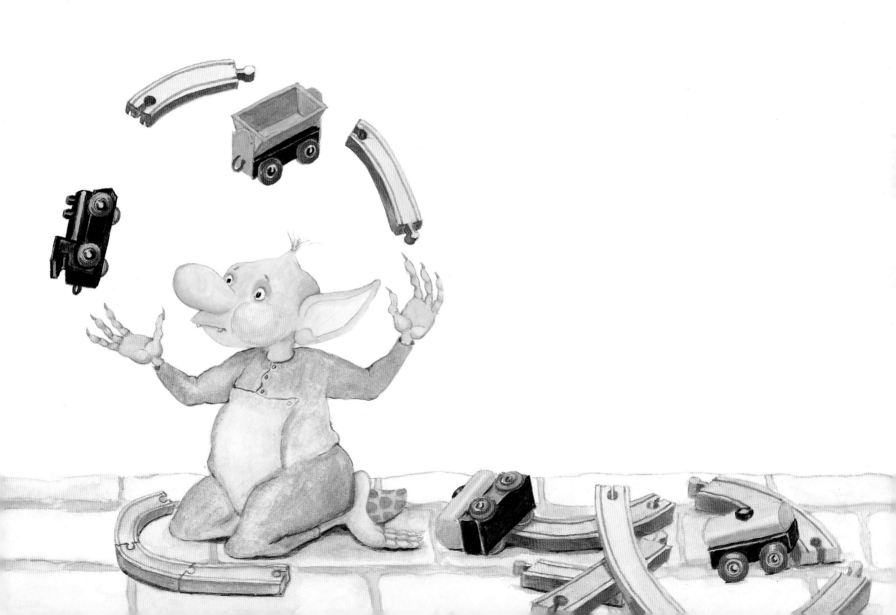

But Billy wanted to sleep in the toy box, too.

"Let Billy have a turn," said Ma and Pa
and Grandma and Grandpa.
"He's only little."

So Billy went to sleep in the toy box.

And Hazel put the train set back together,

and built the bricks up again,

and turned the dolls' house the right way up.

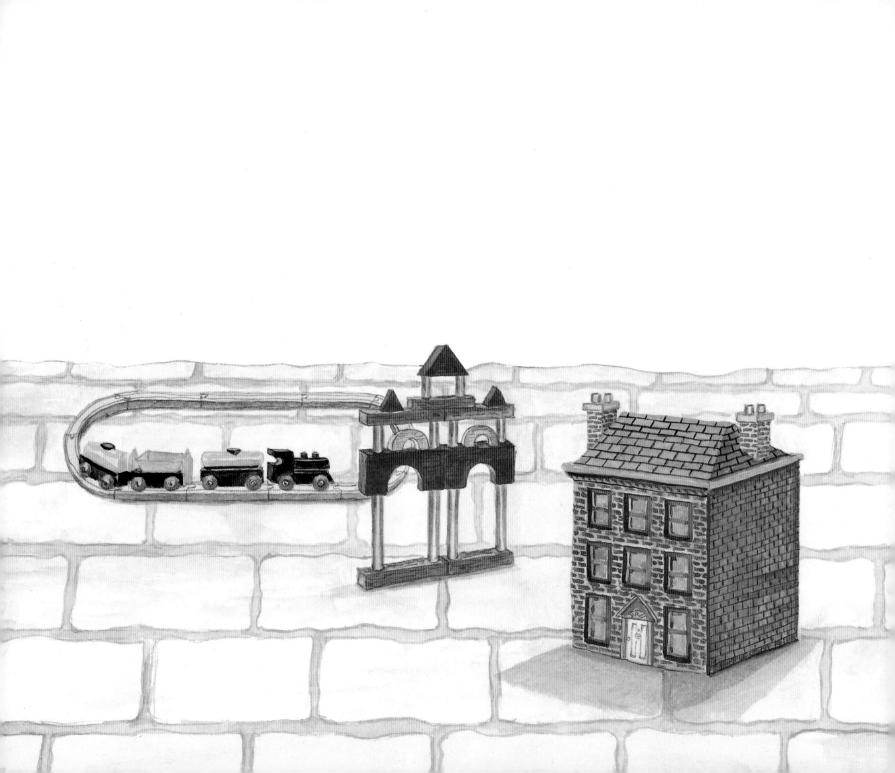

"Silly Billy," said Hazel.

Since the publication of *Rosie's Walk* in 1968, reviewers on both sides of the Atlantic have been loud in their praise of Pat Hutchins's work. Among her popular picture books are *Tidy Titch*; *What Game Shall We Play?*; *Where's the Baby?*; *The Doorbell Rang*; *You'll Soon Grow into Them, Titch*; and *The Wind Blew* (winner of the 1974 Kate Greenaway Medal). For older readers she has written several novels, including *The House That Sailed Away*, *The Curse of the Egyptian Mummy*, and *Rats!* Pat Hutchins, her husband, Laurence, and their sons, Morgan and Sam, live in London.